PAPPY

ANGEL-BABY

PATCH

DECAF

Little Brown

Marla Frazee

Beach Lane Books

New York   London   Toronto   Sydney   New Delhi

For the dogs

BEACH LANE BOOKS

An imprint of Simon & Schuster Children's Publishing Division
1230 Avenue of the Americas, New York, New York 10020
Copyright © 2018 by Marla Frazee
BEACH LANE BOOKS is a trademark of Simon & Schuster, Inc.
For information about special discounts for bulk purchases, please
contact Simon & Schuster Special Sales at 1-866-506-1949 or
business@simonandschuster.com.
The Simon & Schuster Speakers Bureau can bring authors to your live
event. For more information or to book an event, contact the Simon &
Schuster Speakers Bureau at 1-866-248-3049 or visit our website at
www.simonspeakers.com.
Book design by Marla Frazee
The text for this book was hand-lettered by Marla Frazee, and the
illustrations were rendered in black Prismacolor pencil and goauche.
Manufactured in China
0718 SCP
First Edition
10 9 8 7 6 5 4 3 2 1
Library of Congress Cataloging-in-Publication Data
Names: Frazee, Marla, author.
Title: Little Brown / Marla Frazee.
Description: First edition. | New York : Beach Lane Books, [2018] |
Summary: "Little Brown is grumpy and lonely at the dog park, until he
decides to take matters into his own hands."— Provided by publisher.
Identifiers: LCCN 2017045043 | ISBN 9781481425223 (hardcover : alk.
paper) | ISBN 9781481425247 (e-book)
Subjects: | CYAC: Dogs—Fiction. | Mood (Psychology)—Fiction.
| Loneliness—Fiction.
Classification: LCC PZ7.F866 Li 2018 | DDC [E]—dc23 LC record
available at https://lccn.loc.gov/2017045043

Little Brown was cranky.

Probably because no one ever played with him.

Or maybe no one ever played with him
because he was
cranky.

At this point,
    it was hard to know.

The big dogs chased balls.

The small dogs
ran around in circles.

The old dogs napped together in the shade.

The young dogs got muddy.

But Little Brown did nothing and did it alone.

He knew he could be a dog who would — if given half a chance — chase balls, run in circles, nap in the shade, or get muddy.

But Little Brown just watched the others . . .

and got crankier and crankier.

That's why when that ball rolled right over to him,

he nabbed it.

And that's why he grabbed the tassel toy too.

And the blanket.

And the stick.

And the
flying disk.

And the
football.

And the
happy
rope,

the chew bone,

the stripy pillow,   and even

the

rock.

Soon he had
collected quite
   a lot of things
that didn't belong
   to him.

The big dogs and small dogs and old dogs and young dogs stopped what they were doing and looked at Little Brown.

They looked at the stuff.
They wanted it back.

But Little Brown
wasn't giving in.

This was a dilemma.

The dogs wondered
things, some of
which they'd
wondered
before....

Is Little Brown cranky because we don't play with him?
Or do we not play with him because he is cranky?
Should we play with him to get the stuff back?

Little Brown
wondered things
too.

If I give it all back, will they like me?
Then will they play with me?
What if I give it all back and they still won't play with me?
What then?

None of the dogs could figure it out. Neither could Little Brown.

It was a lot to wonder about.

So they all sat around wondering and scratching until it was time to go in.

Maybe tomorrow...

they would know
what to do.

GUS

MARLITA

LAIKA

ROCKET